MENTAL HEALTH GUIDES

UNDERSTANDING
ANXIETY

by Celina McManus

BrightP◈int Press

San Diego, CA

BrightPoint Press

© 2021 BrightPoint Press
an imprint of ReferencePoint Press, Inc.
Printed in the United States

For more information, contact:
BrightPoint Press
PO Box 27779
San Diego, CA 92198
www.BrightPointPress.com

Content Consultant: Michael J. Zvolensky, PhD, Hugh Roy and Lillie Cranz Cullen Distinguished University Professor, Director, Anxiety and Health Research Laboratory/Substance Use Treatment Clinic, University of Houston

LIBRARY OF CONGRESS CATALOGING-IN-PUBLICATION DATA

Names: McManus, Celina, 1992- author.
Title: Understanding anxiety / Celina McManus.
Description: San Diego : ReferencePoint Press, 2021. | Series: Mental health guides | Includes bibliographical references and index. | Audience: Grades 10-12.
Identifiers: LCCN 2020002440 (print) | LCCN 2020002441 (eBook) | ISBN 9781682829837 (hardcover) | ISBN 9781682829844 (eBook)
Subjects: LCSH: Anxiety--Juvenile literature. | Anxiety disorders--Juvenile literature.
Classification: LCC BF575.A6 M386 2020 (print) | LCC BF575.A6 (eBook) | DDC 152.4/6--dc23
LC record available at https://lccn.loc.gov/2020002440
LC eBook record available at https://lccn.loc.gov/2020002441

CONTENTS

AT A GLANCE

- Anxiety is a feeling of worry or uneasiness. It is common and treatable.

- Everyone experiences anxiety. But some people have anxiety disorders. Their anxiety affects their daily lives.

- Anxiety comes with mental and physical symptoms. One common symptom is racing thoughts. Physical symptoms include a rapid heartbeat.

- Generalized anxiety disorder (GAD) is the most common anxiety disorder in the United States. Nearly 7 million US adults have GAD.

- In 2018, 19 percent of US adults had anxiety disorders. That was about 40 million people.

- Some people get panic attacks. A panic attack is a sudden and intense feeling of fear. Some people have panic disorder, a type of anxiety disorder. They experience repeated panic attacks.

- Anxiety disorders can affect people's relationships. They can also affect people's work lives. People who have these disorders often feel tense and exhausted.

- Mental health professionals can treat people who have anxiety disorders.

- There are many ways to treat anxiety disorders. Cognitive behavioral therapy (CBT) is the most common treatment.

WHEN ANXIETY SHOWS UP

Andre clutched his stomach. He was having stomach pains again. It was late at night, and he was in bed. His mom had given him stomach medicine. But it was not helping. His thoughts raced. Andre worried about his pains. He also worried about other things. He was expecting a new baby sister. He was excited to have

Stomach pain is common among people who have anxiety disorders.

a sibling. But he also thought about what

could go wrong. Maybe his sister would not

like him. Maybe his parents would love his

sister more than they loved him.

Many people who have anxiety disorders have sleeping problems. Lack of sleep can make it difficult for people to remember things or learn new information.

Andre also worried about his grades

in school. He was always tired during

class because he could not get enough

sleep at night. He found it hard to focus

on his schoolwork. Doing homework sometimes made him anxious. His stomach would be in knots again. As a result, his grades were slipping.

The next morning, Andre told his mom about his sleepless night. He explained all his worries. Andre's mom took him to the doctor. The doctor asked Andre lots of questions. Then he suggested that Andre might have generalized anxiety **disorder** (GAD). He **prescribed** a medication. The medication could help reduce Andre's anxiety. The doctor gave Andre's mom the phone number of a therapist. Andre was not sure what to think. But it felt good to have some answers.

ANXIETY DISORDERS

Anxiety is a common feeling. Everyone experiences it in some way. But some people have intense anxiety. It affects their daily lives. These people have anxiety disorders. GAD is one of the most common anxiety disorders. People who have GAD may feel restless. They may have trouble focusing on things. They feel like they are always worrying about something.

Anxiety disorders can look and feel different for each person. Each person may

People who have GAD often worry about doing well in school. But their anxiety can make it difficult for them to concentrate.

have a different set of symptoms. There are

also many types of anxiety disorders. It can

be helpful to understand where anxiety

comes from. Luckily, there are ways to treat

anxiety disorders.

CHAPTER ONE

WHAT IS ANXIETY?

Anxiety is a feeling of worry or uneasiness. It comes from fear. Fear is a normal response to a threat. A threat is something dangerous. The brain is wired to respond to danger. The brain is part of the nervous system. It sends signals when a person is in danger. Nerves carry the signals throughout the body. Other parts of

One common fear many people have is a fear of heights. If people avoid many situations because of this fear, they may have an anxiety disorder.

the body respond. This reaction happens

quickly and without thought. For example,

one type of danger could be a spider.

Spiders can bite people. Many people are

afraid of spiders. When they see spiders,

they may run away. This is a reaction from the nervous system. It is an example of a fight-flight-freeze response.

When someone is in danger, extra oxygen is sent to her brain. This helps her stay alert. Her brain tells her heart to beat faster. She starts to breathe faster too. All of her energy is focused on the problem at hand. She may stay and fight the danger. Or she may take flight. This means she runs away. Some people do not react at all. Their mind goes blank. They freeze.

Anyone can have this fear response. But people who have anxiety disorders have this reaction even when there is no danger. They often think about past events that were frightening. They also think about similar events that could happen in the future.

Edmund Bourne is an expert on anxiety. He says, "There are many situations . . . in which it is appropriate and reasonable to

THE BRAIN'S ROLE

Scientists study the amygdala to understand anxiety. This part of the brain is involved in the fear response. It is almond-shaped. It is in the center of the brain. It interprets what people see, hear, and touch. It can sense danger. Then it tells the nervous system that something is wrong.

react with some anxiety."[1] But people who have anxiety disorders feel intense anxiety. They might have panic attacks. Intense anxiety is not as severe as a panic attack. But it is worse than typical anxiety.

WHAT IS A PANIC ATTACK?

A panic attack is a strong feeling of fear. It hits someone suddenly. The person's heart rate increases. The person might have difficulty breathing. Dizziness is another symptom.

Panic attacks may be a sign of panic disorder (PD). But people who have other anxiety disorders may get panic attacks

Blurred vision can be a sign of a panic attack.

too. Deborah Ledley is a psychologist.

She treats people who have anxiety

disorders. She says, "Although panic

attacks are very uncomfortable, there is

nothing dangerous about them. I teach patients to remind themselves of that . . . and to carry on despite feeling anxious."[2]

MENTAL ILLNESS

An anxiety disorder is a type of mental illness. A mental illness affects a person's mood, thinking, and behavior. Physical and mental illnesses are related. A person's physical health may suffer if the person has a mental illness. Also, mental illnesses can have physical symptoms. People who have anxiety disorders might have stomach pains. The stomach is part of the digestive system. This system is connected to the nervous system. The nervous system starts

the fight-flight-freeze response. This takes

up the person's energy. Digestion slows

down as a result. Anxiety disorders often

cause problems with digestion.

ANXIETY AND OTHER ILLNESSES

Anxiety can be linked to other health issues.
For example, people who have asthma may
also have an anxiety disorder. Asthma reduces
airflow to the lungs. This makes it difficult
to breathe. People with asthma may have
panic attacks. Doctors can do tests. The tests
can help them see if the anxiety is related to
another illness. The anxiety disorder may go
away once the illness is treated.

Anxiety can show up in different ways. Sometimes, it seems to come from nowhere. People who have intense anxiety should talk to a medical doctor. Doctors can help people find out if they have a disorder. Doctors often run tests first. The tests help rule out physical illnesses. A doctor may not find anything in the body to explain how a person is feeling. Then the doctor may tell the person to see a mental health professional. Psychologists and other mental health professionals can **diagnose** disorders. They can identify a disorder from its symptoms.

Some psychologists are trained to treat certain groups of people, such as kids. They may work in schools or other types of environments.

TYPES OF ANXIETY DISORDERS

There are many types of anxiety disorders.

Nearly 7 million US adults have GAD. Kids

and teenagers can also have GAD. People

with GAD have ongoing worry. They have

little control over this feeling. They usually have more anxiety in a situation than is typical. For example, they may feel anxious about choosing an outfit.

Some people have illness anxiety disorder (IAD). They believe they have a serious illness. This fear of illness lasts for at least six months. The fear can be caused by normal sensations such as digestion. People who have IAD do not see this feeling as normal. Instead, they see signs of a disease. Their anxiety affects their daily life. They may avoid places that they think could make them sick. It can be hard for

People who have illness anxiety disorder may visit the doctor often.

them to function. They are often distracted.

They may spend hours searching disease

symptoms on the internet. IAD affects about

five percent of Americans.

Six million US adults have PD. Kids

and teens can also have this disorder.

About 20 million Americans have aerophobia, or a fear of flying.

People with this disorder have panic

attacks. They live in fear of these attacks.

They try to avoid situations that trigger

these attacks.

About 15 million US adults have social anxiety disorder (SAD). Kids and teens can also develop SAD. They feel overwhelming anxiety in social situations. Another anxiety disorder that is even more common is phobia. A phobia is a strong fear of something. About 19 million US adults have phobias. Some people are afraid of animals. Others are afraid of certain situations. For example, some people are afraid of heights. These fears affect their daily lives.

Agoraphobia is another anxiety disorder. Nearly 2 million US adults have this disorder. They fear places where escape could be difficult. They feel trapped in these places. They avoid crowded areas such as shopping malls.

It is possible to have multiple anxiety disorders. People with GAD often have other anxiety disorders. People may also have other mental health issues such as depression. Depression is a mental illness. It causes feelings of sadness that do not go away. Depression can develop from an anxiety disorder. For example, someone who has PD may avoid situations that cause panic attacks. They may lose interest in activities they once enjoyed. They may

About 60 percent of people who have anxiety disorders also have symptoms of depression.

also become sad and exhausted from

anticipating a panic attack. Many things

happen in the mind and body as someone

experiences anxiety.

CHAPTER TWO

HOW DOES ANXIETY AFFECT PEOPLE?

Anxiety disorders affect people on many levels. They influence people's moods and thoughts. Certain events or situations bring on the anxiety. These events or situations are called stressors. Everyone experiences stressors of some kind. They are part of life. A stressor can

People who have anxiety disorders often feel distracted or tense.

be a test in school. Public speaking is

another common stressor. People with

anxiety disorders have many stressors.

Their stressors may differ from those

of people who do not have disorders.

They may feel anxious in situations that do not normally cause anxiety. William Meek is a psychologist. He treats people who have GAD. He says, "If you are someone who has more severe anxiety over 'things that shouldn't be a big deal,' it may be more than normal anxiety."[3] In this case, it could be GAD.

TRIGGERS

People with anxiety disorders also have triggers. A trigger is something that causes a strong reaction. People react to familiar senses such as sights and smells. For example, someone may have a panic attack

Some people have panic attacks in crowded areas. They may develop agoraphobia and avoid crowded areas as a result.

in a mall. They may see crowds of people.

They may smell certain foods. They connect

these things to the panic attack. Similar

sights or smells might trigger a panic attack

in the future.

DAILY LIFE WITH A DISORDER

People experience anxiety disorders in different ways. Each person's experience is different. But there are common signs and symptoms. The intensity of a person's anxiety can be a sign of a disorder. Another sign is anxiety that lasts a long time.

People who have anxiety disorders may not be able to get something off their mind. This is called obsessive thinking. For example, people sometimes have to give speeches. People who have SAD would think a lot about the speech. They may not be able to stop thinking about it. They may worry that they will fail or embarrass themselves. This constant worry affects other parts of their lives. They might not be able to sleep. They could have difficulty eating. They might find it hard to focus on anything else.

WHAT CAUSES ANXIETY DISORDERS?

Scientists do not know exactly what causes anxiety disorders. There are many factors. Life experiences are one factor. Physical conditions can play a role too. Anxiety disorders can also run in families. Parents can pass disorders on to their kids. Kids may also learn certain behaviors from their parents. Scientists are studying other possible causes too.

People's brains are on high alert when they are anxious, and their muscles tense up. This can make them feel mentally and physically exhausted.

Other symptoms show up in the body.

People with anxiety disorders may feel

tense. They might feel hot or cold. Their

breathing might quicken. They may also

feel a tightening in their chest. Intense anxiety and panic attacks are exhausting. People who have anxiety disorders often feel tired. They can get lots of rest and still be exhausted.

People try to avoid situations that cause anxiety. Anxiety disorders create a state of constant worry. People who have these disorders get anxious in everyday situations. They try to avoid these situations. In this way, anxiety limits what they can do.

OTHER SYMPTOMS

Each disorder has different symptoms. People who have GAD are anxious for long periods of time. Their anxiety lasts for six months or more. They find it hard to stop worrying. This anxiety makes it difficult for them to do daily activities. They may have

ALICIA'S STORY

Alicia Tatar has GAD. She says, "I've struggled with severe anxiety for as long as I can remember." She started feeling anxious in elementary school. She was later diagnosed with GAD. In middle school, she started going to the nurse every week. She did not feel like eating. She almost failed gym class because she was too nervous to participate. Some teachers called her lazy. Her mom helped her find treatment. She learned healthy ways to deal with her anxiety.

Source: Alicia Tatar, "What Anxiety in Teens Looks and Feels Like: Alicia's Story," Your Teen Magazine, n.d. www.yourteenmag.com.

People who have SAD often fear that others will judge and reject them.

trouble sleeping or focusing. They may also

get angry easily. Other common symptoms

include a sore jaw or back. People often

Panic attacks can feel scary or uncomfortable, but they do not cause any bodily harm.

tighten their jaw and back muscles when they worry. Muscles get sore when they are overused.

People who have SAD experience fear or **stress** when they meet new people. They worry that other people are judging them. They feel anxious when they think people are watching them. For example, they dislike when people watch them eat. Performing can be scary. People who have SAD may avoid social events.

Panic attacks may be a sign of an anxiety disorder. An attack usually lasts ten to twenty minutes. People feel a loss

Anxiety can cause migraines, or severe headaches. Migraines can make people sensitive to light and noises.

of control. The anxiety seems to come

from nowhere. People may think they are

having a heart attack. They might think

they are dying. They may feel sweaty and start to tremble. Panic attacks can cause stomach pain. They often make people feel dizzy and lightheaded. A person's arms and legs may feel numb. The person may also get migraines. Migraines are severe headaches.

People who think they have an anxiety disorder should talk to a doctor or therapist. These professionals know the symptoms of different disorders. They will ask questions to identify if someone has a disorder. Then they can figure out how to treat the person.

CHAPTER THREE

HOW DOES ANXIETY AFFECT SOCIETY?

Anxiety disorders are common among children and young adults. In the United States, nearly one out of three teens develops an anxiety disorder. Many adults also have severe anxiety. In 2018, about 40 million US adults had anxiety disorders.

For some people who have agoraphobia, their anxiety may become so severe that they avoid daily activities such as grocery shopping. They may stay inside their homes for most of the day.

Anxiety disorders do not affect just the people who have them. They also affect friends and family. For example, a child may have a parent who has SAD. The child

People who have anxiety disorders may find it hard to meet deadlines or deal with problems in the workplace.

might want the parent to come to a soccer game. A soccer game is a social situation. So the parent may not go. The child might feel hurt or ignored.

Many people feel stressed or anxious at work. This feeling is worse for people who have anxiety disorders. People with severe anxiety may have difficulty leaving their house. It may be hard for them to go to work. Some workplaces encourage their employees to talk to a therapist. Therapists can help people deal with mental health issues. But not everyone talks openly about their anxieties. Many people with anxiety disorders feel ashamed.

Anxiety disorders are the most common type of mental illness in the United States. In 2019, more than half of US college students asked for help with anxiety

problems. But some people still do not seek

the help they need. In 2018, only 37 percent

of people who were diagnosed with anxiety

disorders received treatment. There are

many reasons why people might not

SCREEN TIME

Smartphone use and anxiety are linked.
As time spent on smartphones increases,
so does anxiety. Many people check social
media through their smartphones. People with
anxiety disorders tend to use social media
often. They do this to distract themselves.
But people compare themselves to others when
they use social media. This can make them feel
more anxious.

seek treatment. A major reason is that some people think mental illnesses are shameful. Many people have mental illnesses. There is no shame in being ill. Still, this belief persists. Shame can prevent people from seeking help. They may not want to admit they have a mental illness. Other people's attitudes can make it difficult for them to ask for help. Many people misunderstand mental illness. Groups such as the National Alliance on Mental Illness (NAMI) share information about this topic. They raise awareness of mental health issues.

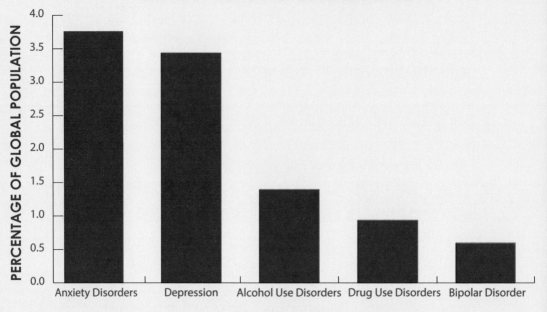

MENTAL HEALTH DISORDERS IN 2017

Hannah Ritchie and Max Roser, "Mental Health," University of Oxford, April 2018. www.ourworldindata.org.

In 2017, 797 million people around the world had a mental health disorder. This graph shows some of the most common disorders in that year.

PRESSURE AND DISCRIMINATION

Many people feel pressure from society.

American society values success and

hard work. In 1985, the Higher Education

Research Institute (HERI) did a survey.

HERI interviewed new college students from more than 1,000 universities. HERI asked if they felt stressed. Eighteen percent said yes. HERI did a follow-up survey in 2016. By then, the number had increased. Forty-one percent said yes.

School can also be scary for people who experience **discrimination**. They may be bullied because of their identities. Twice as many **LGBTQ** youth report being bullied compared to straight students. Cole Ledford is a gay activist. He raises awareness of mental health issues among LGBTQ people. He lives with an

People who are bullied have a higher risk for developing anxiety disorders as well as other mental health issues.

anxiety disorder. He has panic attacks.

He shares his experiences. He says,

"I think that [sharing] just allows people to

see a real human experiencing that, and

surviving that."[4]

In 2017, 60 percent of LGBTQ youth said they felt sad or hopeless most of the time. This percentage is highest among transgender youth. Trans people do not identify with the sex assigned to them at birth. They face anxiety over basic issues. For example, a trans boy may want to use the men's bathroom. But the school may not let him use this bathroom. The school may want him to use the bathroom that matches the sex he was assigned at birth. So it may make him use the women's bathroom.

Anxiety disorders are more common among certain groups of people. African Americans are more likely to have severe stress than white people. They may experience discrimination. Discrimination causes stress. Even some doctors discriminate against African Americans. They provide better treatment to white

MORGAN'S STORY

Morgan is a teenager. She is transgender. She went to private schools. These schools expected her to act like a boy. This made her anxious. She was also depressed. She wanted to be seen as a girl. She felt guilt and shame. Then she received medical help for her mental illnesses. She found supportive people.

people than to black people. They may ignore a black patient's symptoms.

Discrimination can lead to **poverty**. The poverty rate among African Americans is high. People who live in poverty have little money. Money problems create stress and anxiety. Angela Neal-Barnett is an African American psychology professor. She studies mental health in black communities. She says, "What I have discovered . . . is that African Americans have not had a name for what they were experiencing."[5] She sees that people are often ashamed to talk about these issues.

African Americans are more likely to distrust their doctors and less likely to visit hospitals than white people.

COSTS

Medical treatment is expensive. People with anxiety disorders may have insurance. Insurance can help with the cost. But they often have to pay for much of the treatment themselves.

There are taxes to help fund mental health care. Anxiety disorders cost the United States more than $42 billion each year. Medical expenses can be high. Hospitalization for a mental illness can cost up to $10,000. It can be hard for people to make these payments. The main reason

Anxiety and stress can cause nightmares.

people do not seek treatment is because

they cannot afford the cost.

SEEKING HELP

Anxiety disorders affect society in many

ways. They affect how people live.

For example, a group of men attacked Maria when she was fifteen years old. She was walking to school. For months, Maria kept thinking about the attack. She had nightmares. She could not walk to school on her usual route. The anxiety affected her daily life. Then she decided to tell someone about her experiences. She talked to her art teacher. Her art teacher helped her. Maria started seeing a therapist. It is important for people with anxiety disorders to seek such treatment.

CHAPTER FOUR

HOW IS ANXIETY TREATED?

Mental health professionals help treat anxiety disorders. There are many types of mental health professionals. Therapists and counselors offer counseling. Counseling is a type of treatment. It helps people deal with mental health issues. People create goals. They work toward these goals. This helps them get better.

Some therapists provide family therapy, a treatment that involves talking to clients and their families. Family therapy can help people who have anxiety disorders.

Therapists can include psychologists

and psychiatrists. Psychologists help

people learn what causes their anxiety.

They help people change their thoughts

and behaviors. Psychiatrists are doctors.

They can prescribe medicine. They can also

run tests and do physical exams.

THERAPY

Therapy is another form of treatment.

Therapists are trained to provide this

treatment. They try to reduce or get rid of

MENTAL HEALTH AWARENESS

Many people know that mental health is important. But some people do not get the help they need. One in five Americans is afraid to seek help because of shame. But many groups are working to change this. Mental Health Awareness Month happens each year in May. Groups raise awareness of mental health issues.

a person's symptoms. The type of therapy treatment depends on the person and the disorder.

Cognitive behavioral therapy (CBT) is the most common treatment for anxiety disorders. CBT helps change people's thinking patterns and behaviors. It teaches people coping skills. These skills help them deal with stressors.

There are two kinds of coping skills. The first is emotion focused. The second is problem focused. In some cases, people want to change their thoughts about a situation. They need emotion-focused

CBT helps people change their thinking patterns so they can cope with the symptoms of a panic attack.

coping skills. For example, people may

think they are dying when they have a panic

attack. But they can remind themselves

that they will get through it. They can

try distracting themselves. These are

emotion-focused coping skills. Chuck

Schaeffer is a psychologist. He suggests,

"Visualize each feeling as a wave. . . .

Anticipate the wave passing and becoming

less and less intense."[6]

Problem-focused coping skills are

also helpful. People learn how to change

the situation itself. They might remove

something stressful from their lives. They

also learn to ask others for support.

Exposure therapy is another part of

CBT. It can help people who have anxiety

disorders. Therapists ask people to imagine

fearful situations. This can help people face

Some people have claustrophobia, a fear of enclosed spaces. People who have claustrophobia or agoraphobia may not like being in elevators.

their fears. For example, someone may have

a phobia. He may be afraid of elevators.

The therapist will ask him to imagine being

in an elevator. Then the therapist may ask

him to look at pictures of elevators. The last

stage of the process may be going into an elevator. Over time, his anxiety in this situation may be reduced. This is the goal of exposure therapy. Misti Nicholson is a psychologist. She explains, "When we avoid panic or treat it like an enemy, we make it stronger. . . . I often encourage my patients to do the opposite of what anxiety

VIRTUAL REALITY

Therapists may use virtual reality (VR) in exposure therapy. VR involves computer technology. A computer creates a virtual situation. The situation reflects a person's fears. For example, VR can help people who have SAD. In their VR situation, they may be in front of a crowd. Everyone may be looking at them. Therapists help them face their fears.

is expecting them to do. This often means moving toward what they are afraid of."[7]

People may need to see a therapist for several weeks. Therapists help people find the therapies that work best for them. Most therapies help people figure out the source of their anxiety.

MEDICATION

Medication can also help people who have anxiety disorders. It reduces their symptoms. Medication works best when paired with therapy. Medication can help for a short time. Therapy helps people in the long term.

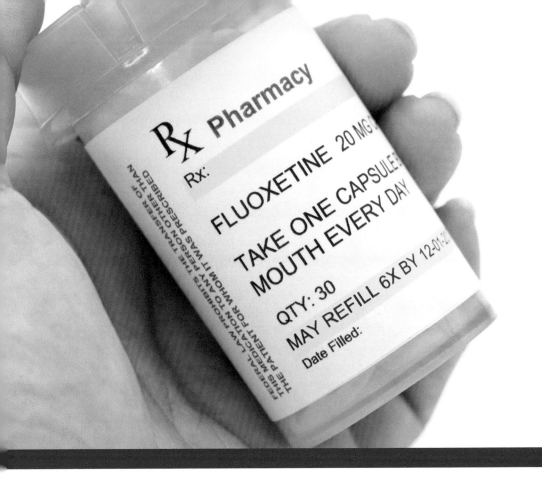

Fluoxetine is a medication that can be used to treat PD.

There are many types of medications.

Each person's body and mind are different.

A medication that works well for one person

might not work for another person. Also,

someone may have to try many medications

before finding the right one. This is always done with the help of a professional.

Some medication helps keep people's moods stable. It can increase serotonin levels. Serotonin is a chemical. Nerve **cells** make it. It controls a person's moods. People with anxiety disorders may have low levels of serotonin. This makes it hard for them to manage their fear. It can also make it difficult for them to fall asleep. Medication can help.

COPING STRATEGIES

People who have anxiety disorders should monitor their thought patterns. They should

Journaling can help people identify things that make them anxious or stressed.

examine their fears. They should think about

where these fears come from. Writing these

thoughts in a journal helps. People can

learn more about their thought processes

when they journal.

Meditation can also help relieve anxiety. Meditation is a way to focus on thinking processes. People remove themselves from distractions. They focus on their breathing. They often close their eyes. They pay attention to their body. Meditation is about mindfulness. Mindfulness is a way of being accepting of oneself. It is an awareness of thoughts and feelings. This can help reduce anxiety. Meditation is often paired with a mantra. A mantra is a repeated phrase or word. It helps redirect people's thoughts. That way, people stop thinking about their anxiety.

People can learn how to meditate through guided meditation.

Support groups or group therapy may help some people who have anxiety disorders.

Meditation does not work for everyone.

But people can be mindful of their

breathing. This is important for people who

have anxiety disorders. Deep breathing

slows a person's heartbeat. The person's muscles relax.

Anxiety disorders are common. But they are treatable. There are many treatment options. Today, people are raising awareness of anxiety disorders. With their help, more people may seek treatment in the future.

GLOSSARY

cells

the building blocks of all living things that help them function and grow

diagnose

to identify an illness or condition based on its symptoms

discrimination

the act of treating people differently based on their race or other characteristics

disorders

physical or mental conditions that affect a person's ability to function and cause distress

LGBTQ

a term used to refer to lesbian, gay, bisexual, transgender, and queer people

poverty

the condition of being poor or lacking resources

prescribed

wrote a prescription, or an official recommendation that tells someone which medicine to take

stress

a feeling of pressure or tension

SOURCE NOTES

CHAPTER ONE: WHAT IS ANXIETY?

1. Quoted in "Everything You Wanted to Know About Anxiety—From an Expert," *New Harbinger Publications*, May 11, 2018. www.newharbinger.com.

2. Quoted in "Get to Know LifeSpeak Expert and Psychologist Dr. Deborah Ledley," *LifeSpeak*, n.d. www.lifespeak.com.

CHAPTER TWO: HOW DOES ANXIETY AFFECT PEOPLE?

3. William Meek, "The Difference Between Normal Anxiety and GAD," *Verywell Mind*, November 23, 2019. www.verywellmind.com.

CHAPTER THREE: HOW DOES ANXIETY AFFECT SOCIETY?

4. Quoted in Mark O'Connell, "Pride In Mental Health: An Interview With LGBT Activists, Cole Ledford and Dior Vargas," *HuffPost*, July 14, 2017. www.huffpost.com.

5. Quoted in Mashaun D. Simon, "A Look at How Anxiety Affects African-Americans," *NBC News*, January 31, 2018. www.nbcnews.com.

CHAPTER FOUR: HOW IS ANXIETY TREATED?

6. Quoted in Nicole Spector, "What to Do (and Carry with You) to Cope with a Panic Attack," *NBC News*, May 29, 2018. www.nbcnews.com.

7. Quoted in Nicole Spector, "What to Do (and Carry with You) to Cope with a Panic Attack."

FOR FURTHER RESEARCH

BOOKS

Holly Duhig, *Understanding Anxiety*. New York: PowerKids Press, 2019.

Jennifer Lombardo, *Anxiety and Panic Disorders*. New York: Lucent Press, 2018.

Hilary W. Poole, *Anxiety and Fear in Daily Life*. Broomall, PA: Mason Crest, 2018.

INTERNET SOURCES

"A Student with Social Anxiety on Why a First Impression Isn't Always Enough," *PBS News Hour*, August 22, 2019. www.pbs.org/newshour.

"Anxiety: When You Are Worrying About Things," *Women's and Children's Health Network*, June 28, 2018. www.cyh.com.

"Anxiety Disorders," *KidsHealth*, March 2014. www.kidshealth.org.

"Yoga: Meditation and Breathing," *KidsHealth*, n.d. www.kidshealth.org.

WEBSITES

The Anxiety and Depression Association of America (ADAA)

www.adaa.org

The ADAA provides information and resources for people who have anxiety or depression. It also helps people find treatment.

The HEARD Alliance

www.heardalliance.org

The HEARD Alliance shares resources for youth who have depression and related mental health conditions. It provides the phone numbers for mental health hotlines. It also helps youth find mental health providers.

The National Alliance on Mental Illness (NAMI)

www.nami.org

NAMI's website has information about mental illnesses. It also offers support and a hotline people can call.

INDEX

IMAGE CREDITS

Cover: © fizkes/Shutterstock Images

5: © tommaso79/iStockphoto

7: © AaronAmat/iStockphoto

8: © Photographee.eu/Shutterstock Images

11: © Monkey Business Images/Shutterstock Images

13: © verbaska_studio/iStockphoto

17: © Tero Vesalainen/Shutterstock Images

21: © Africa Studio/Shutterstock Images

23: © Monkey Business Images/Shutterstock Images

24: © Ilya Studio/Shutterstock Images

27: © Suzanne Tucker/Shutterstock Images

29: © Motortion Films/Shutterstock Images

31: © Xavier Arnau/iStockphoto

34: © Antonio Guillem/Shutterstock Images

37: © fizkes/Shutterstock Images

38: © Pixel-Shot/Shutterstock Images

40: © Prostock-studio/Shutterstock Images

43: © tommaso79/Shutterstock Images

44: © fizkes/Shutterstock Images

49: © Red Line Editorial

50: © Daisy Daisy/Shutterstock Images

54: © Rocketclips, Inc./Shutterstock Images

56: © Marcos Mesa Sam Wordley/Shutterstock Images

59: © Lisa F. Young/Shutterstock Images

62: © Alpha Prod/Shutterstock Images

64: © Pixel-Shot/Shutterstock Images

67: © Sherry Yates Young/Shutterstock Images

69: © Wayhome studio/Shutterstock Images

71: © ESB Professional/Shutterstock Images

72: © pixelheadphoto digitalskillet/Shutterstock Images

ABOUT THE AUTHOR

Celina McManus writes poetry, fiction, and children's literature in the Twin Cities. She is an MFA candidate at Randolph College. Her work is featured or forthcoming in *Women's Art Quarterly Journal*, *Hooligan Magazine*, and *Rabid Oak*. When she isn't writing, you can find her in a body of water with any pal who may join her.